PHINEAS L. MACGUIRE . . .

GETS COOKING!

For Win Hill and Gavin Schulz,
two of my favorite geniuses

The author would like to thank the most fabulous Caitlyn Dlouhy and the most marvelous Ariel Colletti for being utterly fabulous and marvelous, and she wants to give a big tip of the hat to Lyn Streck, science teacher extraordinaire. Thanks to Kaitlin Severini, pretty much the best copy editor ever, and to Sonia Chaghatzbanian, the most marvelous book designer. Thank you to the fantastic Laura Ferguson for all of her fantastic work, and lots of love and gratitude to the usual gang of family and friends who keep the author centered and sane, which is no easy job.

Also by Frances O'Roark Dowell

Chicken Boy • *Dovey Coe* • *Falling In* • *The Kind of Friends We Used to Be* • *Phineas L. MacGuire . . . Blasts Off!* • *Phineas L. MacGuire . . . Erupts!* • *Phineas L. MacGuire . . . Gets Slimed!* *The Second Life of Abigail Walker* • *The Secret Language of Girls* *Shooting the Moon* • *The Sound of Your Voice, Only Really Far Away* • *Ten Miles Past Normal* • *Where I'd Like to Be*

atheneum

ATHENEUM BOOKS FOR YOUNG READERS • An imprint of Simon & Schuster Children's Publishing Division • 1230 Avenue of the Americas, New York, New York 10020 • This book is a work of fiction. Any references to historical events, real people, or real places are used fictitiously. Other names, characters, places, and events are products of the author's imagination, and any resemblance to actual events or places or persons, living or dead, is entirely coincidental. • For information about special discounts for bulk purchases, please contact Simon & Schuster Special Sales at 1-866-506-1949 or business@simonandschuster.com. • The Simon & Schuster Speakers Bureau can bring authors to your live event. For more information or to book an event, contact the Simon & Schuster Speakers Bureau at 1-866-248-3049 or visit our website at www.simonspeakers.com. • Book design by Sonia Chaghatzbanian • The text for this book is set in Garth Graphic. • The illustrations for this book are rendered in pencil. • Manufactured in the United States of America • 0913 OFF • First Edition • 10 9 8 7 6 5 4 3 2 1 • CIP data for this book is available from the Library of Congress • ISBN 978-1-4814-1462-3 • ISBN 978-1-4814-0101-2 (eBook).

FROM THE HIGHLY SCIENTIFIC NOTEBOOKS OF PHINEAS L. MACGUIRE

PHINEAS L. MACGUIRE . . .

GETS COOKING!

PART TWO: BROWNIES SOOTHE THE SAVAGE BEAST

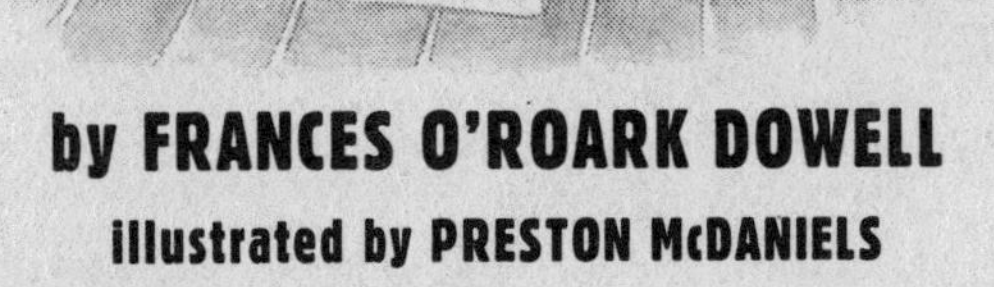

by FRANCES O'ROARK DOWELL

illustrated by PRESTON McDANIELS

Atheneum Books for Young Readers

New York London Toronto Sydney New Delhi

PREVIOUSLY IN

PHINEAS L. MACGUIRE . . .
GETS COOKING!

Phineas L. MacGuire., scientist extraordinaire, has been tasked with cooking the family dinner! Despite his uncertainty toward learning how to cook, it turns out that it is actually a lot like chemistry: add ingredients and watch cool (and yummy) things happen! Phineas and his friends, Aretha and Ben, are in the midst of deciding what dessert could win the big bake-off (and the $10,000 prize) when Evan Forbes, the school bully, starts demanding a batch of Phineas's brownies every day before school. Phineas has to keep up, or get clobbered. It's time to cook up a plan!

OIL

"Let me explain to you how mayonnaise works. Have you ever heard of a colloid?"

Aretha's dad, Mr. Timmons, stood at the kitchen counter with a food processor in front of him. Aretha, Ben, and I were sitting on tall kitchen stools on the other side of the counter. We were taking notes in our notebooks, and Ben was filming. "I don't want to miss any important information," he'd explained when he showed up at Aretha's with his camera. "Plus, who knows? Maybe we could end up doing our own cooking show. 'Aretha's Dad Teaches Kids to Cook,' something like that."

"I don't know about a colloid," Ben said now. "But I've heard of a collard. Is that the same thing?"

Mr. Timmons laughed. "Not quite. You make a colloid when you dissolve one thing into another thing. When we're talking about liquids, it's more accurately called an emulsion."

Aretha and I both wrote like crazy in our notebooks. Ben popped off his chair so he could move in for a close-up.

Holding up an egg and a bottle of olive oil, Mr. Timmons said, "The interesting thing about mayonnaise is, here you have two things that don't typically mix. You've got your oil, and in this egg you have water. But because we're going to *slowly* dissolve the oil into the eggs, we're going to bring these two opposites together."

Then he broke three eggs into the food processor and punched the on button. Once the eggs were all mixed up, he started dripping olive oil into the feed tube on top.

"You have to be patient," Mr. Timmons told us. "Just a little bit of oil at a time."

It seemed like it took forever, but all of a sudden the stuff in the food processor turned all creamy and white.

"Cool!" Ben exclaimed, recording the mayo from all angles. "There's only one problem."

"What's that?" Mr. Timmons asked.

"Mayonnaise sort of makes me feel sick."

Mr. Timmons nodded. "Me too, but I know you guys are interested in science, and this is the most food science I know. So who wants to learn how to make hamburgers for lunch?"

We'd already made scrambled eggs, hard-boiled eggs, omelets, and egg salad (which was when Mr. Timmons decided he should to teach us how to make mayonnaise). To be honest, I was getting a little tired of eggs. Hamburgers sounded great.

After Mr. Timmons gave us all his best hamburger cooking tips (don't overhandle the meat, fry the burgers in butter, don't turn up the heat too high), and we had four burgers frying in a pan, Aretha said she thought we should have salad with our burgers in order to keep our meal nutritionally balanced. "One thing I'm supposed to do for my badge is make a meal healthier," she told us. "Adding a salad in this situation will definitely do the trick."

Mr. Timmons gave Aretha the thumbs-up. "Salad dressing is the easiest thing in the world," he said, handing me the olive oil and a bottle of balsamic vinegar. "Two parts oil to one part vinegar, and you've got salad dressing. All you've got to do is put it in a jar, put the lid on, shake the jar up, and there you have it—your very own colloid!"

"But since it's liquid, we call it an emulsion,"

Aretha said, writing in her notebook. "Right?"

"You got it, my little genius," Mr. Timmons said. "Now who wants to peel some carrots?"

After we finished eating lunch, me, Ben, and Aretha cleaned up the kitchen and tried to brainstorm egg recipes, but it turned out everybody was sick of eggs.

"How about an omelet with bacon and raspberries?" Ben asked as we were getting ready to leave. "Or a BLT omelet?"

"I don't think you can cook lettuce," Aretha told him. "It gets all slimy."

"You could use spinach instead of lettuce," I suggested. "People eat slimy spinach all the time. I mean, you know, the cooked stuff."

Of course, at our house, you'll find most of the slimy spinach in a bag at the bottom of the vegetable bin in the fridge.

That, you want to avoid.

When I got home, I decided to study my lab notes from my week of kitchen duty. Since I'd started cooking dinner, I'd learned a lot of stuff.

First, there were all the lessons I learned about making spaghetti the first night. The next day, when I made the brownies for Evan, I learned about the importance of cleaning up as you go, or else you won't actually have time to make dinner. Last night, when I'd finally gotten around to trying homemade waffles, I learned that a tablespoon is not a spoon you'll find on a table, but an actual measuring spoon that's with all the other measuring spoons in the kitchen drawer.

Which might explain why my waffles came out sort of flat.

"Kind of like tortillas," Lyle had observed when I served them up. "Except with syrup."

It was my mom who figured out I'd used a cereal spoon to measure out the baking powder. "That would give you about a teaspoon of baking powder," she explained. "And the recipe called for a tablespoon, so three times as much. Baking powder is a leavening agent. Do you know what that means?"

"Leavening agent?" I asked. My mom raised

her eyebrows—the universal signal in our house for "look it up."

So I looked it up. A leavening agent is what makes stuff puff up by producing carbon dioxide. I already knew about yeast, but it turns out that baking powder and baking soda are leavening agents too. Without them, cookies, waffles, bread, and cake would all fall flat.

Lesson learned.

Reading my lab notes, I felt like I'd had a pretty good week, even if I hadn't made anything explode yet. I knew deep down that exploded food probably wouldn't taste all that good, but I bet it was the funnest food to cook.

So if my week had been so scientifically successful, why did I have a bad feeling in the pit of my stomach?

Two words: Evan Forbes.

I'd made two batches of brownies already for Evan, and next week he wanted me to make him three. "I'm selling some of them to my buddies," he explained. "Fifty cents a pop. I'm raking in the dough, Mac."

To be honest, that didn't seem very fair to me. I was doing all the work. Why should Evan be making all the money?

Unfortunately, I didn't have the guts to ask him.

One thing I knew for sure was that Sarah was going to start getting suspicious if I made brownies nearly every afternoon. And if Sarah got suspicious, she'd start nosing around and figure out that Evan Forbes was a brownies bully. Then she'd tell my mom, and my mom would call Principal Patino, and Principal Patino would call Evan into the office, and then after school Evan would clobber me.

I needed a plan.

Fortunately, I was a scientific genius, so it only took me eight hours to come up with one. I was brushing my teeth, and I was thinking about what I was going to do the next day. Ben wanted me to come over to his apartment so we could work on our prizewinning recipe. He still didn't know what he wanted to make, and we needed to decide fast.

I thought about what Aretha said. Make something you like, but make it a little bit different. Give it a new twist.

Well, I liked brownies, or at least I used to like brownies before Evan Forbes started forcing me to bake them.

So why not work on a fantastia-zoid brownie recipe? That would give me just the excuse I needed for making a ton of brownies. I could make fifty brownies a day and start stockpiling them in the freezer. By the end of the week, I might have enough brownies to give Evan for the rest of the year.

I'm a genius, I thought, spitting toothpaste

into the sink. I bet there were a million ways to make brownies. Brownies with chocolate chips, brownies with marshmallows, brownies with broken-up peppermint candies.

And, okay, sure. Why not? We could even try brownies with bacon.

"Brownies are kind of boring, don't you think?" Ben was sitting on the couch in his apartment, drawing a new Derek the Destroyer comic book and watching Saturday morning cartoons. Derek the Destroyer is this superhero Ben made up a couple of years ago. In spite of his name, he's actually a good guy, and he's always saving the world from total annihilation. In the most recent series of Derek the Destroyer comics, Earth is under attack by an army of giant mold monsters who slime everything in their path as they fight for world domination.

It's totally cool.

"Boring? Brownies?" I shook my head like I couldn't believe how dumb Ben was being. "They're like the most exciting dessert product ever. They're practically a dessert *event.* Thick, rich, moist, chocolaty. Plus, they're easy to make, and I bet we could come up with an original recipe that will blow the judges' socks off."

Ben thought about this for a minute. "I wonder if we could come up with a brownie recipe that you could set on fire. Like, there's this dessert called cherries jubilee, and right before you serve it, you make it burst into flames."

"How do you do that?"

Ben shook his head. "I'm not sure. I guess you pour something on it that flames up and then burns out."

"And isn't poisonous," I added.

"Right. We can find out. Brownies jubilee. That has a nice ring to it, don't you think?"

I actually thought flaming brownies sounded like a great idea, but I was pretty sure that wasn't the direction I wanted to go in. Evan Forbes would definitely clobber me if I gave him burned-up brownies. "Maybe we should start with some simpler recipes and build up to brownies jubilee," I said. "Perfect our recipe and then add special effects to it."

"That's probably a good idea," Ben agreed. "I'll just go call Mrs. Klausenheimer, and we can get started."

"Why do you have to call Mrs. Klausenheimer?"

"In case you haven't noticed, my mom's at work, which means we are currently semi-unsupervised. My mom said if we even thought about turning on the oven, we had to call Mrs. Klausenheimer to come over and be the official adult."

Ben lives in an apartment building. His mom is the apartment building manager. Most of their neighbors are old people, and a couple of months ago when we did a dog slobber experiment, we went around to different apartments to get slobber samples. Mrs. Klausenheimer's dog was one of the scariest ones we met, a huge German shepherd with teeth the size of baseball bats.

Very sharp baseball bats.

"She's not going to bring Killer with her, is she?"

Ben looked worried. "I don't think so. Chocolate is really bad for dogs. She probably doesn't want to take the chance that he'll eat a bunch of brownies and have to go to the vet."

Five minutes later there was a knock on the door. "Bennie! I'm here!"

When Ben opened the door, Mrs. Klausenheimer shuffled in clutching an overstuffed purse and headed directly for the couch. "Now, you're making brownies, is that right? I know the most divine recipe. It calls for eggnog, whipped cream, and crème de menthe. Does your mother keep those things in her pantry, Bennie?"

"I don't think so, Mrs. Klausenheimer," Ben told her. "She mostly keeps normal stuff."

"Too bad, too bad." Mrs. Klausenheimer pulled a copy of *Celebrity Homes and Recreation Vehicles* magazine out of her purse. "Well, you boys run along and make your brownies. Don't get your fingers caught in the mixer!"

"She's our official adult?" I whispered as I followed Ben to the kitchen. "She's like the opposite of Sarah Fortemeyer. You could get away with anything!"

"I know, cool, right?" Ben asked with a grin. "Sometimes she babysits me, and we order six pizzas with all different kinds of toppings. Then we have a contest to see who can eat the most slices. After that, Mrs. Klausenheimer falls asleep and I can do whatever I want."

Sometimes I think Ben's the luckiest kid in the world.

All the ingredients for basic brownies were lined up on the kitchen counter. I grabbed my backpack, which I'd thrown on the kitchen table earlier. "So I figure we have time to try three different kinds," I told Ben, dumping the contents of my backpack out on the table. "First, M&M's brownies. Second, marshmallow brownies. And third—"

"I got it!" exclaimed Ben. "Pizza brownies. Genius-zoid! Why didn't I think of that earlier! Pepperoni, mozzarella, delicious!"

"Yeah, except for the part where you start throwing up. Pizza brownies? Are you serious?"

"Perfectly serious," Ben said with a perfectly serious expression on his face. "Everybody loves pizza, everybody loves brownies. Why not combine the two?"

"I mentioned the part about throwing up, right?"

Ben shrugged. "I think you underestimate people, Mac. It's the twenty-first century. We eat all kinds of stuff now!"

I could see that Ben was not going to be budged unless I figured a way to work around him. "Okay, how about this? We call the M&M's pepperoni, the marshmallows mozzarella, and for the tomato sauce . . ."

"Actual tomato sauce! It's sweet, right? It'll work, Mac, I'm telling you!"

"No, it won't," I said. "You have to trust me on this. But maybe we could chop up some maraschino cherries?"

Ben sniffed a couple of times, like the idea sort of offended him, but then he gave in. "Yeah, I think we have some maraschino cherries in the fridge," he admitted.

"Okay, we'll do pizza brownies first," I told him. "And then we'll try a couple of other kinds."

"Do you think we're going to start getting sick of brownies?" Ben asked.

I was already sick of brownies, but I couldn't admit that without explaining the Evan Forbes situation. So I kept my mouth shut.

By the end

of the afternoon, we had seventy-two brownies. The pizza brownies were okay, but Ben thought the next time we tried them, we ought to use marshmallow cream instead of marshmallows, spread it over the top of the baked brownies, and then put the M&M's and maraschino cherries on top.

My favorite brownies were the ones that just had marshmallows in them. Simple, gooey, delicious, and nothing at all like pizza.

"They're all fantastic, boys," Mrs. Kleisenheimer said when she woke up from her nap and sampled one of each. "Next time with the M&M brownies, add some more M&M's. You can never have too many M&M's, in my humble opinion."

"The question is, which ones will the judges like best?" Ben scratched his chin. "How does a recipe judge think? I like the pizza brownies a lot, but they need one more element. Something else that will really make them stand out."

"We could make them explode," I suggested.

Ben jumped about five feet in the air. "Exploding Pizza Brownies! Fantastizoid! Incredibaloo! Yes, Mac! Yes!"

I'm pretty sure he liked the idea.

I liked it too. I liked it especially when I thought about a brownie exploding right as Evan Forbes was about to take a bite.

Ben thumped me on my back. "You're a genius, Mac. I've always said it."

"But I don't actually know how to make exploding brownies," I told him. "That could be a problem."

"How hard could it be?" Ben said with a shrug. "You mix in a little of this, a little of that, and whammo! Exploding brownie! Easy peasy."

"Maybe if we added bacon to the brownie mix, we could have sizzling brownies," I said. "Sizzling is almost as good as exploding."

"Sizzling and exploding are two entirely different things," Ben argued. "Still, you might have a point. A little bacon in our brownies could really make the flavor pop."

Okay, so maybe our brownies wouldn't explode, but they could definitely pop. Popping was a step in the right direction.

I just hoped Evan Forbes liked bacon.

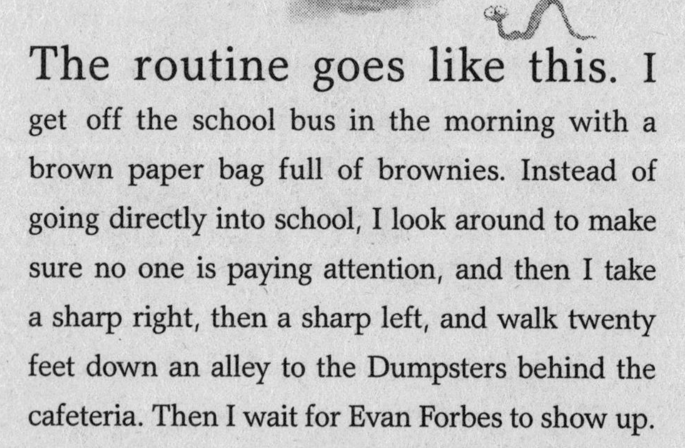

The routine goes like this. I get off the school bus in the morning with a brown paper bag full of brownies. Instead of going directly into school, I look around to make sure no one is paying attention, and then I take a sharp right, then a sharp left, and walk twenty feet down an alley to the Dumpsters behind the cafeteria. Then I wait for Evan Forbes to show up.

The Dumpsters are the stinkiest part of the school. I don't mind stinky stuff as much as other people do, because bad smells are a sign that some science is happening. In fact, spending so much time around the Dumpsters got me thinking. So why does stuff stink in the first place?

Here is what my research has turned up:

1. Stuff that stinks is usually stuff you shouldn't eat. So stinkiness may be nature's way of telling you to stay away so you won't eat something and immediately croak.
2. Some stinky things are actually okay to eat, like Limburger cheese, which stinks because of the bacteria that's used to make it. It's called *Brevibacterium linens,* which is the same bacteria that makes people stink if they haven't taken a shower in a while.
3. Just because it's okay to eat Limburger cheese doesn't mean I'm going to.
4. I mean, have you ever
5. A lot of stinky stuff is in the process

of decomposing. Tissues are breaking down and bacteria are eating everything they can get their hands on, which produces the gas that makes us plug our noses.

6. Bacteria are responsible for a lot of the world's stinkiness.

So maybe I'm being bullied into making brownies every day, but at least I'm getting to learn some interesting new science facts.

On Monday I stood by the Dumpsters, holding a bag with a dozen marshmallow brownies. I hoped Evan liked marshmallows. When I heard someone walking down the alley toward the Dumpsters, I automatically started worrying that Evan Forbes hated marshmallows, and my stomach started hurting like crazy because I thought this might be the day that he finally clobbered me.

It was only a matter of time.

"Mac?"

The voice was familiar, but it wasn't Evan's.

Mr. Reid came around the corner of the Dumpsters. "What are you doing back here, Mac? This area is off-limits to students."

"I was—uh—I was—just waiting."

"Waiting for what?"

"For a friend of mine." I held out the bag. "I wanted to give him some of the brownies I made this weekend. Me and Ben are working on a recipe for this contest. If we win, we're going to each get five thousand dollars. I was thinking I might use my five thousand dollars to buy a chemistry set. Do you know anything about chemistry sets, Mr. Reid? Because I sure could use some advice—"

Mr. Reid cut me off. "Whoa there, Mac! Your mouth is going a hundred miles an hour, and I still can't figure out what you're doing here. Why would you meet a friend behind the Dumpsters to give him brownies?"

I couldn't think of an answer.

"Well?" Mr. Reid said.

"I like how it smells back here?" I said.

Which, you have to admit, was not a total lie.

Mr. Reid gave me a concerned, grandfatherly-type look. "Mac, what's going on? I saw you out here once last week too. Is there something you want to tell me about?"

I wanted like anything to tell Mr. Reid about the Evan Forbes brownie situation. There was only one problem: I also wanted to live to be ten.

A lot of grown-ups will tell you that if you have a problem, you should tell an adult that you trust. Adults are there to help you. And I pretty much believe this, except in situations where someone will probably kill you if you tell.

I mean, what are the grown-ups going to do? Put Evan Forbes in jail? No, he's a kid, and all they'll do is talk to him and maybe make him stay after school for a week. And he'll make a big deal about how sorry he is, and how he'll never bully another kid again, and then guess what?

He'll clobber me.

Finally I came up with a big lie to tell Mr. Reid. "The thing is—and I kinda know this is against the rules—but I'm playing this spy game with some kids? And the brownies are like a cover? And this is one of our secret spy ring meet-up places?"

"You don't sound too sure of yourself, Mac," Mr. Reid said, looking doubtful.

"I guess I'm just worried I'm going to get in trouble."

Mr. Reid seemed to think about this. "I'll tell you what, Mac. I won't take you to Principal Patino's office this time, but I don't want to find you out here again. Is that understood?"

I nodded. "I promise."

"Then run on inside," Mr. Reid said, smiling, like everything was okay now.

But everything was definitely not okay. First of all, as I walked back up the alley to the front of the school, Evan Forbes showed up.

"Hey! Where are you going with my brownies? I thought I told you to meet me at the

Dumpsters. Well, hand 'em over, dude. And tomorrow, wait until I get here. Understood?"

"I can't," I told him. "Mr. Reid caught me standing there. He says he'll take me to the principal's office if he catches me again."

Evan grabbed the bag from me. "That's your problem, Big Mac. See ya tomorrow."

I slumped against the side of the building. I felt really, truly awful. I was lying to everybody, I was either going to get clobbered or sent to detention, and it was starting to look like I was going to have to give Evan Forbes brownies for the rest of my life.

I closed my eyes. "What am I going to do?" I asked out loud, like I hoped the wall would give me some advice.

When I opened my eyes, Aretha was standing in front of me. "I don't know, Mac. What are you going to do? I can tell you one thing—you need to do something, and fast."

I stared at her. "How much do you know?"

"Everything, I think." She glanced to her left,

and then to her right, like a character in a spy movie. "I've been keeping an eye on you, Mac. It's never a good thing when Evan Forbes starts paying too much attention to a kid. I figured he was up to something, so I've been spying."

"I don't even know how I got into this mess," I told her. "Two weeks ago my life was completely normal."

We started walking to the front of the building. "Yeah, you definitely have a problem, Mac," Aretha said. "An Evan Forbes–size problem."

"So what do I do about it?"

"You meet me and Ben at the jungle gym at recess. With my great brain, your scientific know-how, and Ben's creativity, we'll figure something out."

And just like that, my stomach stopped hurting.

We found Ben dangling upside down from the top bar of the jungle gym.

"Jeez, Mac," he said when Aretha and I explained the situation. "Epic fail on the number one rule in the *The Big Book of Best Friend Rules*, buddy."

"Uh, the what?"

"*The Big Book of Best Friend Rules*. Keeping a secret is the number one no-no."

"I didn't know there was a *Big Book of Best*

Friend Rules," I said, climbing up to the top and taking a seat next to him.

Ben tapped his head. "I keep it all up here. Rule number one: No secrets. Rule number two: Best friends stick together, even if it causes bodily harm."

Aretha pulled herself up so she was dangling from the bar across from me. "I bet if you stood up to Evan, he'd back off. My mom says that most bullies are all talk."

"And so what if he punches you?" Ben added. "He's not going to punch you every day for the rest of your life. I predict three days' worth of punches, tops. Then it's over and you go back to your regular life."

"This isn't making me feel better, guys." I leaned back and looked at the sky. To the west, I saw a bunch of nimbostratus clouds, which meant it would probably rain later.

I thought it was sort of awesome that I knew that fact.

"I wish I could just do science all the time,"

I told Ben and Aretha. "I wish I didn't have stupid problems that I don't know how to solve."

"I know! Maybe you should think of Evan Forbes as a scientific challenge!" Aretha said, her voice all of a sudden excited. "You formulate a question, do your background research—"

"Construct a hypothesis," I continued, "test your hypothesis through experiments, and then analyze your data and draw a conclusion."

"And then eat a doughnut," Ben finished up. "Because what you guys are describing sounds like a lot of work. You're gonna need a doughnut when you're done. Probably one with frosting and sprinkles."

"What we're describing is the scientific

method," Aretha informed him. She pulled herself up so she was sitting on top of the jungle gym and turned to me. "So what's the question you're going to start with?"

I thought about it for a minute. "How about, 'What's the best way to stop a bully from bullying you?'"

Aretha nodded. "That's good. Now, how about research?"

"I could read some articles on the Internet," I said. "And maybe ask Mrs. Patino and Mr. Reid. They've probably seen a lot of bullies over the years."

"You could ask other kids, too," Ben said. "Everybody's got at least one story about somebody being mean to them."

"Yeah! Remember how you were mean to Chester Oliphant at the beginning of the school year?" I asked Ben. That was back in the days when Ben was new to the school and acted like he didn't care if anyone liked him or not.

Ben's face turned red. "I don't want to think

about that. It's sort of embarrassing."

"But it could be helpful to our research!" Aretha exclaimed. "Why *were* you so mean to Chester?"

"I don't know," Ben said with a shrug. "I was just acting all stupid and stuff. I didn't know what else to do."

Later, during social studies, Ben passed me a note. When I unfolded it, I saw he had written in big letters at the top of the paper FOR SCIENTIFIC

RESEARCH ONLY. READ AND DESTROY!

Then there was this list that was titled "Why I was Stupid and Sort of Mean When I First Moved Here."

1. I was scared other people would be mean to me first.
2. Everyone was sort of ignoring me.
3. Chester Oliphant is the only kid in our class shorter than I am.
4. I missed my dad.

Ben's list gave me an amazing idea. I could put together a questionnaire and give it to all the kids in my class. It could be questions for kids who had been bullied and questions for kids who'd been bullies. Most of the kids in my class were pretty nice, but looking around I saw one or two who were friendly now, but had been sort of mean in second or third grade. Also, there were girls like Stacey Windham, who could be super nice to her friends one day and then totally ignore them the next day. Why couldn't she be nice every day?

All of a sudden, I felt better than I had in forever. That's the great thing about science, in my opinion. When you take the scientific approach, instead of sitting around all day feeling rotten about a problem, you look it straight in the eye. You ask questions. You get to the bottom of things.

I was copying down the homework assignment, when a question popped into my mind. What would happen if I told Evan Forbes I wasn't going to bring him brownies anymore?

My hypothesis? I'd get clobbered.

But here's the weird thing: My next thought was, maybe I should do an experiment.

Maybe I should tell Evan Forbes no.

My stomach started hurting just by thinking that. But it didn't hurt as bad as it usually did when I thought about Evan. The thing about me and Evan Forbes was, we were like a colloid. We were two things that didn't really mix together unless you forced them to. We were mayonnaise. We were whipped cream (which, in case you're wondering, is a gas dissolved into a liquid). We were gelatin (solid dissolved into a liquid, FYI).

Now, some things when you force them together turn out okay.

And some things, like me and Evan, are a disaster.

Scientifically speaking, I was pretty sure it was time for us to go our separate ways.

Okay, then. When I got home, I'd do the following:

1. Come up with a list of questions about bullying to hand out to all the kids in my class.
2. Brainstorm all the horrible things that could happen to me if I stopped giving Evan Forbes brownies.
3. Come up with a deadline for no longer giving Evan Forbes brownies.

4. Try not to think too much about getting clobbered when I stop giving Evan Forbes brownies.
5. Make dinner.

I thought about the stuff I could make for dinner. I could make hamburgers and salad, or waffles or spaghetti. I could try a new recipe, liked baked chicken and mashed potatoes.

I leaned back in my chair, starting to get hungry as I pictured all the good things we could eat that night.

And that's when I got my craziest idea ever.

I could invite Evan Forbes over to eat. I could do my scientific research in the comfort of my very own home.

That's too crazy, I thought. Besides, what would be the point? So Evan Forbes could bully me in front of my family? So he could find things to make fun of, like Margaret's potty training chair that Sarah kept parked in front of the TV?

And then this funny picture came into my

head. Remember that day Evan got held back at lunchtime because he hadn't turned in his homework? I'd sort of forgotten about it, but all of a sudden I remembered how his face looked when I turned around, like he was about to cry.

Maybe Evan Forbes wasn't so tough after all. I'd invite him over and see if I could find out.

Evan Forbes sounded confused when I called him that afternoon.

"You want me to do what?"

"Come over to my house for dinner," I said, my voice sounding sort of squeaky. "I'll be cooking. I mean, you seem to like my cooking a lot, right?"

"Yeah, I guess—I mean, no! I mean, you're such a dweeb, MacGuire! People don't go over to other people's houses for dinner!"

"You mean your family never goes to

anybody else's house to eat?"

"My parents work late every night. My nanny makes me dinner."

Evan Forbes had a nanny?

"You have a nanny?"

"Well, she used to be my nanny. Now that I'm older, I guess she's my—I don't know. Whatever you call someone who takes care of you and drives you around and stuff."

"Your assistant?" I thought Evan might like the sound of that.

He did.

"Yeah, my assistant! That's it. She's kind of like my assistant and my personal chef. She cooks dinner every night. So why would I eat dinner someplace else?"

I had to think about that for a minute. "Because it's interesting to try new food and to see how other people live?"

Evan snorted. "You think I want to see how a dweeb like you lives, MacGuire? You're totally gonzo."

"I'm a pretty good cook," I halfway lied. I was pretty much a brownie expert by now, but other stuff? Not so much. "What kind of stuff does your assistant make for dinner?"

"I don't know," Evan said. It sounded like he was stalling. "You know, frozen stuff that you microwave. Pita pockets. Chicken nuggets." He paused. "What are you making for dinner tonight?"

"I was thinking about some baked chicken and mashed potatoes."

"And biscuits?"

I could practically hear Evan sniffing the air, like the smell of biscuits was coming through the phone.

"Yeah, sure," I told him. "I could try some biscuits."

"Okay, whatever," Evan said. "I'll be there at six. But it better be good, MacGuire!"

As soon as I hung up the phone, I yelled for Sarah. "I need help!"

Sarah rushed into the kitchen. "What's

wrong? Did you hurt yourself?"

"Worse! I need to make biscuits, and I don't know how!"

Sarah grinned. "Have no fear! My hundred-year-old granny was a champion biscuit maker. I know all the tricks."

"Really?" I couldn't believe my good luck.

"No, not really. My grandmother's sixty-four and never cooked a day in her life. But my dad makes biscuits for breakfast on Sundays. It's easy peasy."

After that, Sarah started bossing me around. Get the flour! We need baking soda and baking powder! Don't forget the salt!

"And we'll need to make buttermilk," she told me. "So get out the milk and the lemon juice from the fridge."

"How about the butter?" I asked.

"There's no butter in buttermilk," Sarah said. "Buttermilk is the sour milk left over after butter's been churned."

"We're putting sour milk in the biscuits?"

Sarah nodded. "It'll give your biscuits a little zing, Mac. Trust me."

I have never trusted Sarah Fortemeyer a day in my life.

"The thing about buttermilk is that it's not something you usually keep around," Sarah said. "So it's easier just to make a buttermilk substitute by putting a little lemon juice in your milk to curdle it."

"This is not sounding delicious," I told her.

"What did I say, Mac? You've got to trust me on this. I know what I'm talking about."

We added one tablespoon of lemon juice to a cup and a half of milk and let it sit for five minutes. The weird thing was, when we looked at the milk after five minutes, it was kind of clumpy.

"That's because it's curdled," Sarah explained. "The lemon juice separates the milk into curds."

"What does that mean exactly?" I asked, but Sarah shrugged, like she didn't know.

So of course I had to look it up.

Remember how, on Saturday, we learned

about colloids and emulsions? What I learned today was, curdling is like the opposite thing. When something is curdled, the emulsion or the colloid gets separated again. In this case, it's the lemon juice that's breaking stuff up.

If only I could figure out how to curdle me and Evan Forbes.

It didn't take very long to make the biscuits. Sarah let me use the food processor to mix up the butter, flour, baking soda, baking powder, and salt.

"The trick to good biscuits is to not over-handle your dough," she explained. "I'm sure there's a scientific reason for that, but I don't know what it is. What I know is, if you use a food processor to mix up your dry ingredients with your butter, it's faster than doing it by hand, and your biscuits turn out softer."

After we were done mixing the butter and flour, we dumped it in a bowl, and then dumped the buttermilk into the flour. The buttermilk was all lumpy and bumpy, and I was doing some serious trusting that Sarah knew what she was talking about, because right now I was thinking these biscuits might taste pretty gross.

Sarah showed me how to roll out the dough and use a glass to cut out the biscuits. We baked them for eight minutes and then brushed them with melted butter when they were done.

Here is what I learned: Freshly baked biscuits smell better than anything in the world. They are the opposite of stinky. They are in an entirely different universe from stinky.

I couldn't believe I was going to be wasting them on Evan Forbes.

Neither could my mom.

"You invited someone to dinner?" she practically screeched when I told her that Evan would be here at six. She'd just walked in the door, and I thought I'd better break the news to her right away. "Mac, I'm exhausted! And the house is a mess. And who is this Evan Forbes, anyway? I've never heard of him."

"He's this kid from school," I explained.

"And he thinks it's kind of—uh—neat that I'm learning how to cook."

"I've got an idea," my mom said, setting down her briefcase and looking through the day's mail. "He can come over on Saturday. We could make homemade pizza. I've been wanting to try that, and it could be a lot of fun to do it with some friends."

"I think he's really looking forward to biscuits."

My mom looked at me. "You made biscuits?" She sniffed the air. "You made biscuits!"

It was like she morphed into an entirely new person.

It turned out that freshly baked homemade biscuits held powers far beyond those of mortal men.

My mom took a deep breath. "Okay, Mac, Evan can come over. It sounds like you've done a lot of work to make a nice dinner."

"And he doesn't get a home-cooked meal very often," I said. I thought it couldn't hurt to soften my mom up a little more. "His parents aren't ever home for dinner the way you and Lyle are. His nanny just heats him up chicken nuggets."

"Oh, that poor child," my mom said. She came over to me and gave me a hug. "You're very sweet for inviting him to eat with us."

I shrugged. "I like to be a good friend when I can."

What I liked was not getting clobbered. Maybe if Evan Forbes liked my biscuits, he wouldn't feel like clobbering me so much.

Or maybe he'd make me start bringing him biscuits every day instead of brownies.

My stomach started hurting again. Do you

know why your stomach hurts? Sometimes it's from excess gas because you ate something like beans that have a lot of fiber and take longer to digest.

And sometimes it's because your stomach fills up with acid that your body has produced because your brain has told it to be afraid.

To be really honest, I was tired of being afraid.

Anyway, it was time to make the mashed potatoes.

Mashed potatoes are super easy to make, by the way. You peel four or five potatoes and chop them into chunks. Then you boil the chunks for about fifteen minutes, until they're nice and soft. All that's left to do after that is pour in about half a cup of milk, and some butter and salt, and get mashing. I wanted to use the electric mixer, but my mom thought it would be safer to use the hand masher.

I didn't mind. It took my mind off the Evan Forbes problem.

Actually, it kind of gave me an Evan Forbes solution. Mashing potatoes takes awhile, and while I was mashing I started thinking about other stuff, like what questions I was going to ask on my bullying research questionnaire.

That's when I had a genius thought—I was going to have my very own, live bully right there in my house.

I could get Evan to help me come up with questions. I mean, who would know better what questions to ask about bullying than a genuine bully?

Genius!

Or crazy.

I was pretty sure it was one or the other.

PHINEAS has invited Evan Forbes to dinner to figure out *why* Evan is a bully. Maybe if Evan likes Phineas's homemade biscuits he'll forget about the brownies he demands from Phineas every morning. *Maybe* it will even make them friends. But is that a good thing? Phineas isn't sure, but it's the only plan he's got. Hopefully he can solve the Evan problem soon, because Ben and Aretha have some crazy cooking ideas for the bake-off . . . if Phineas doesn't step in soon there will be bacon on top of everything and exploding brownies on the ceiling!

FIND OUT IN THE NEXT INSTALLMENT OF

PHINEAS L. MACGUIRE . . .

GETS COOKING!

PART THREE: A RECIPE FOR DISASTER!

FRANCES O'ROARK DOWELL is the bestselling and critically acclaimed author of *Dovey Coe*, *The Second Life of Abigail Walker*, *Chicken Boy*, *Falling In*, *Where I'd Like to Be*, *The Secret Language of Girls*, and of course, the Phineas L. MacGuire series. She lives with her husband and two sons in Durham, North Carolina.

Connect with Frances online at FrancesDowell.com.